PONGO

Jesse Hodgson

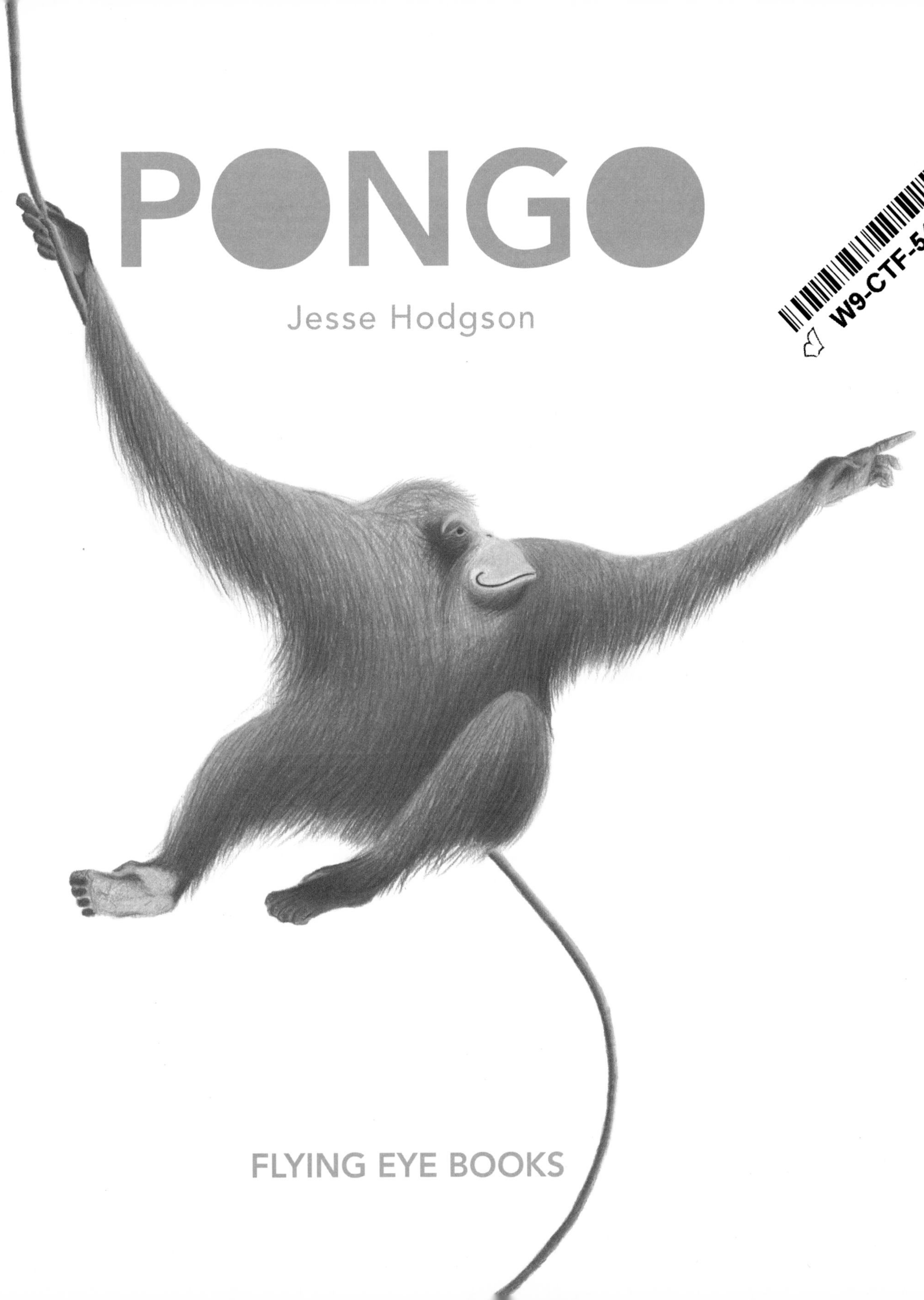

FLYING EYE BOOKS

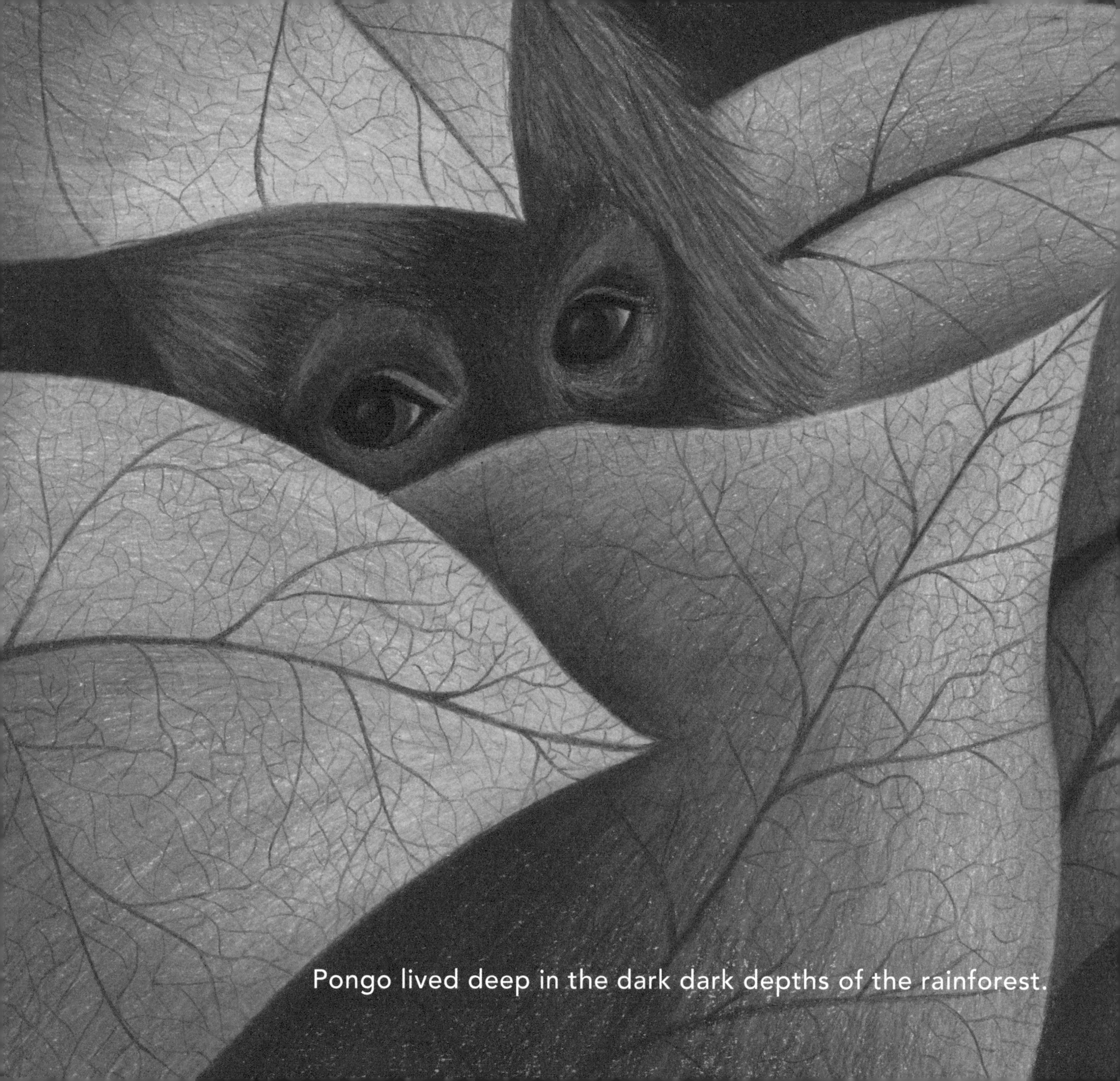

Pongo lived deep in the dark dark depths of the rainforest.

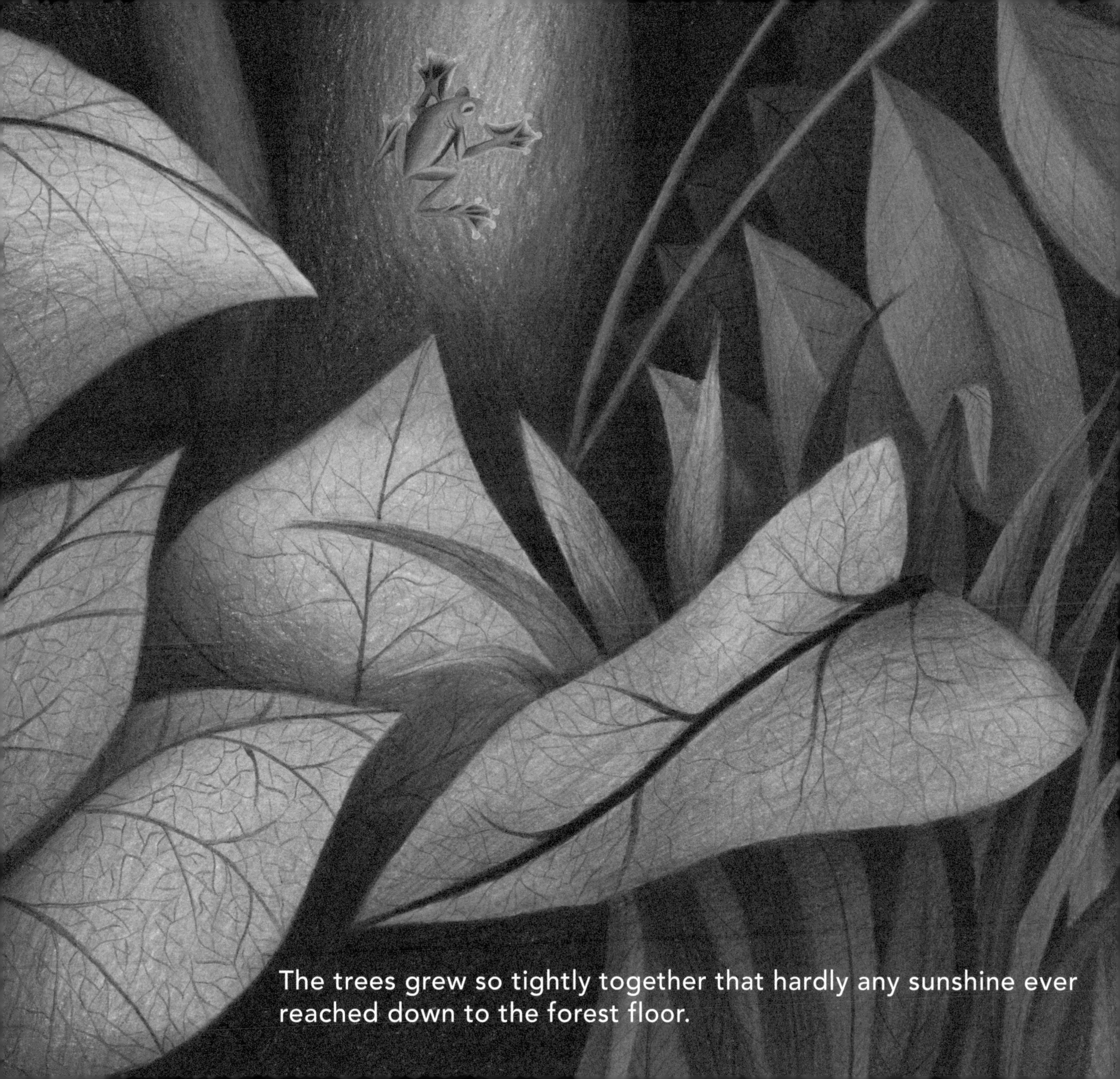

The trees grew so tightly together that hardly any sunshine ever reached down to the forest floor.

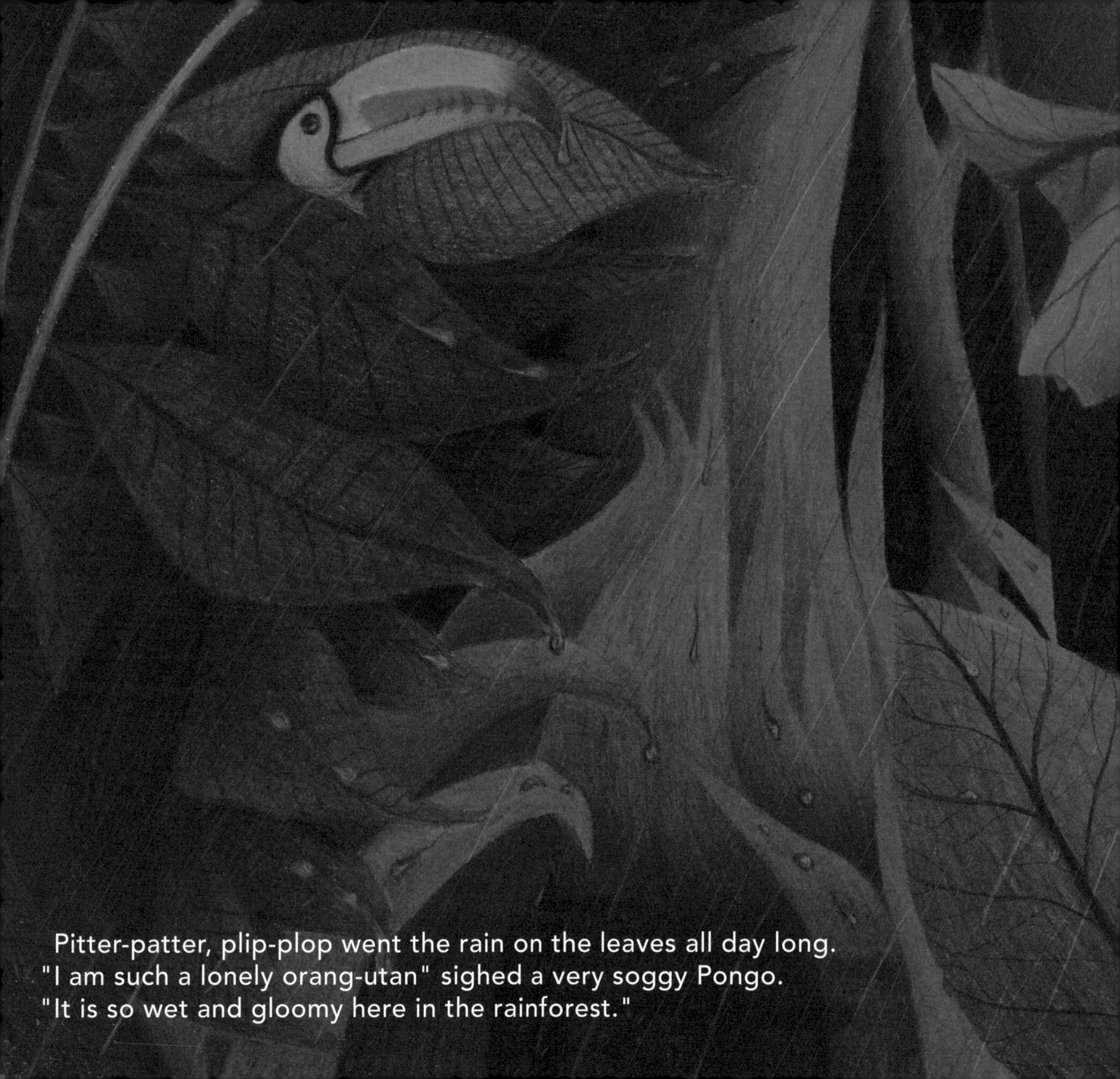

Pitter-patter, plip-plop went the rain on the leaves all day long.
"I am such a lonely orang-utan" sighed a very soggy Pongo.
"It is so wet and gloomy here in the rainforest."

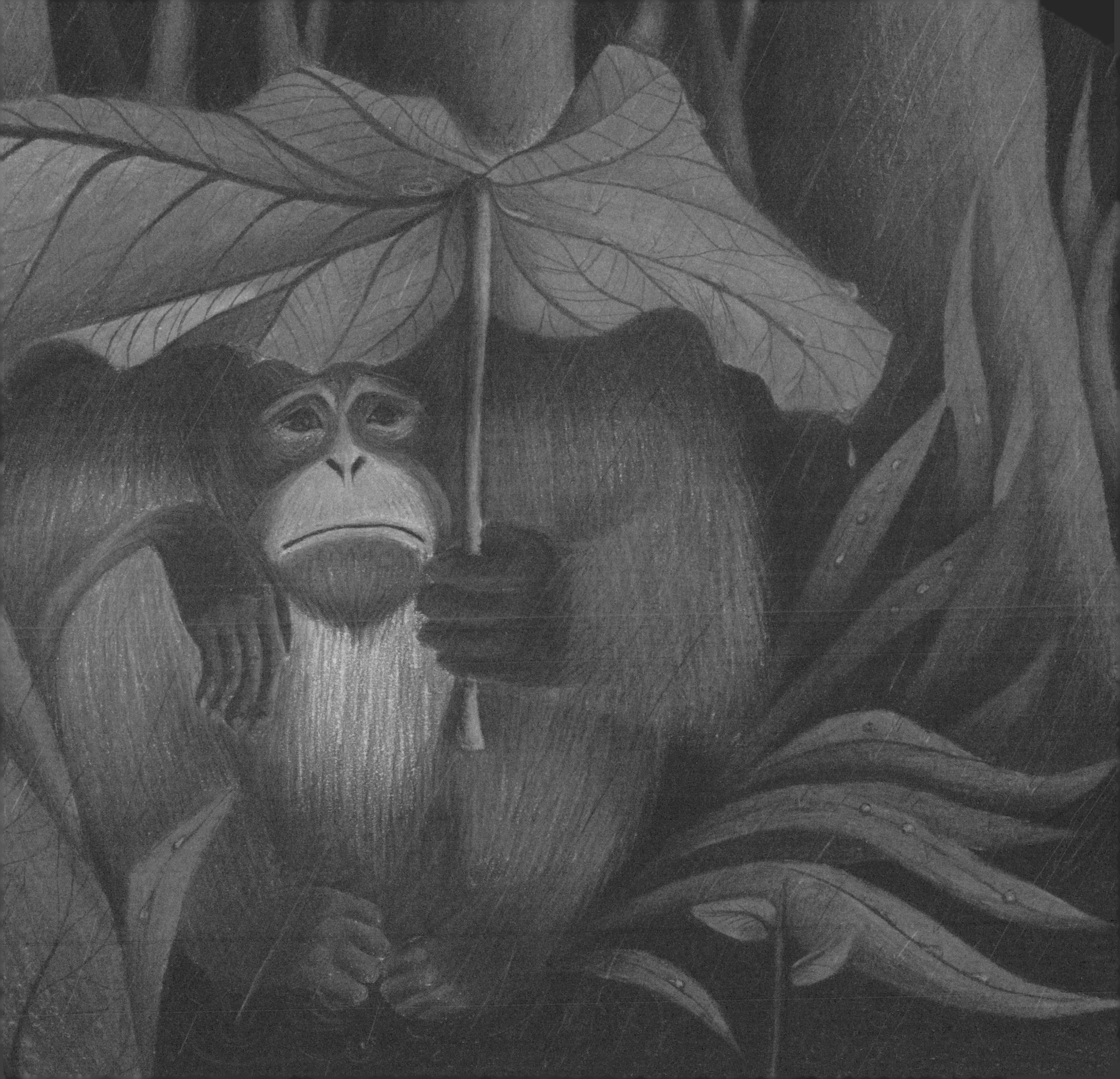

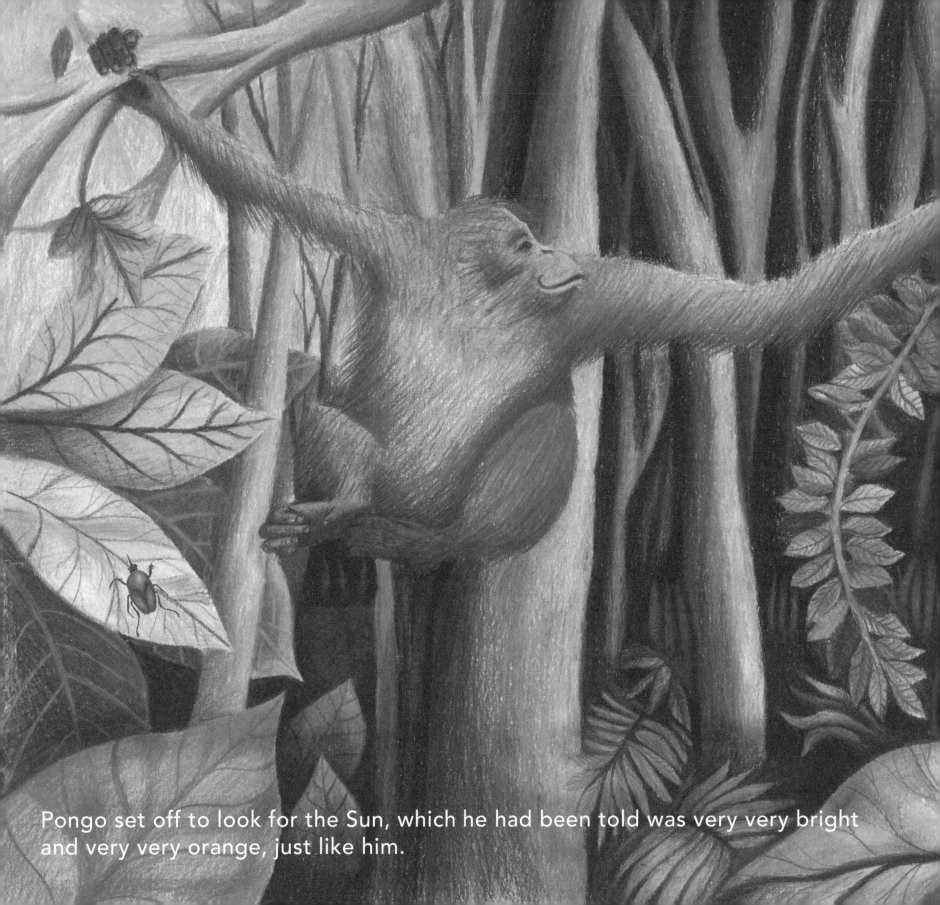

Pongo set off to look for the Sun, which he had been told was very very bright and very very orange, just like him.

"There it is!"

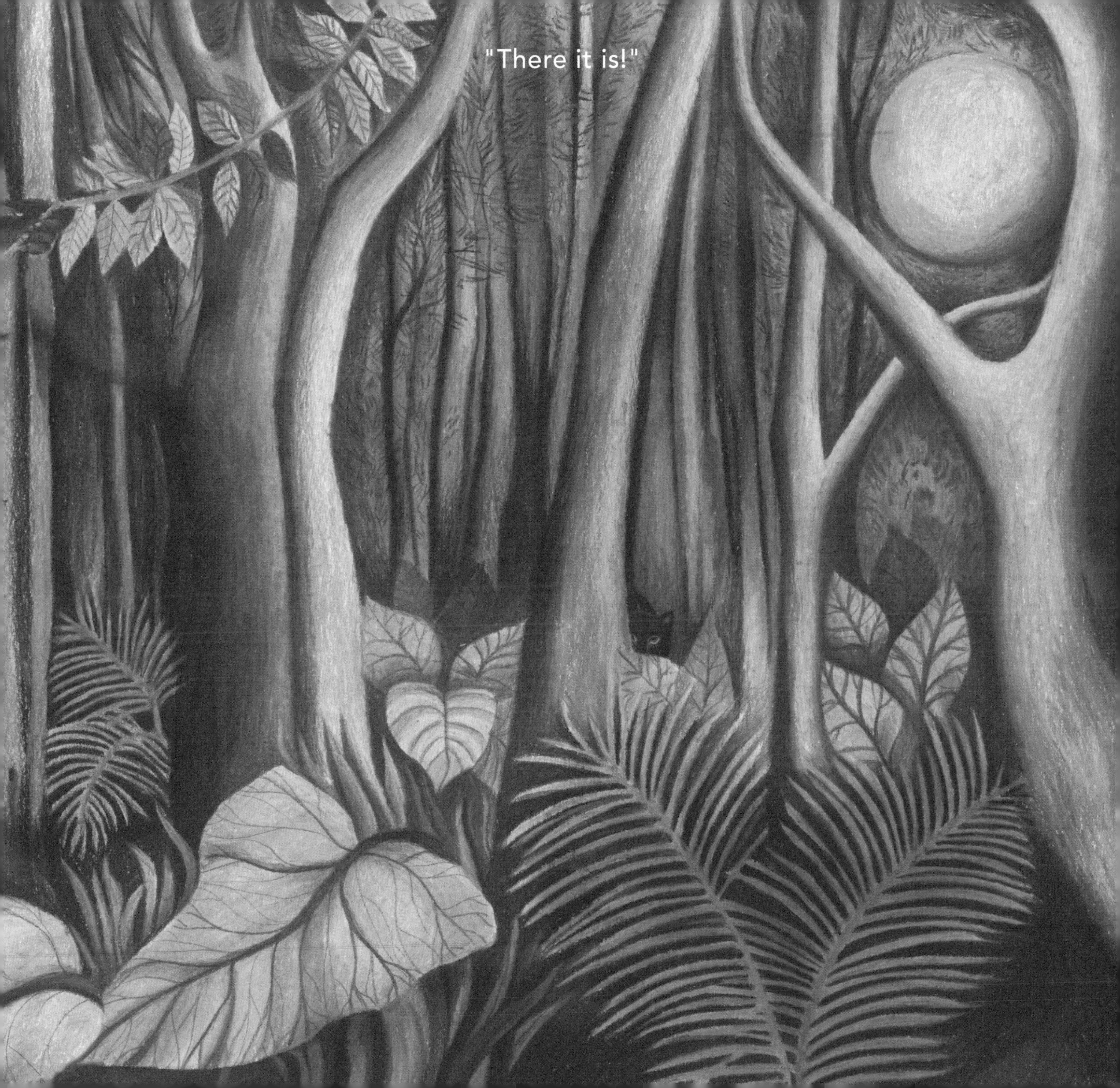

"Who disturbs my ssslumber?" hissed a sleepy snake.
"Excuse me" said Pongo, "are you the Sun?
You are certainly very very bright and very very orange!".

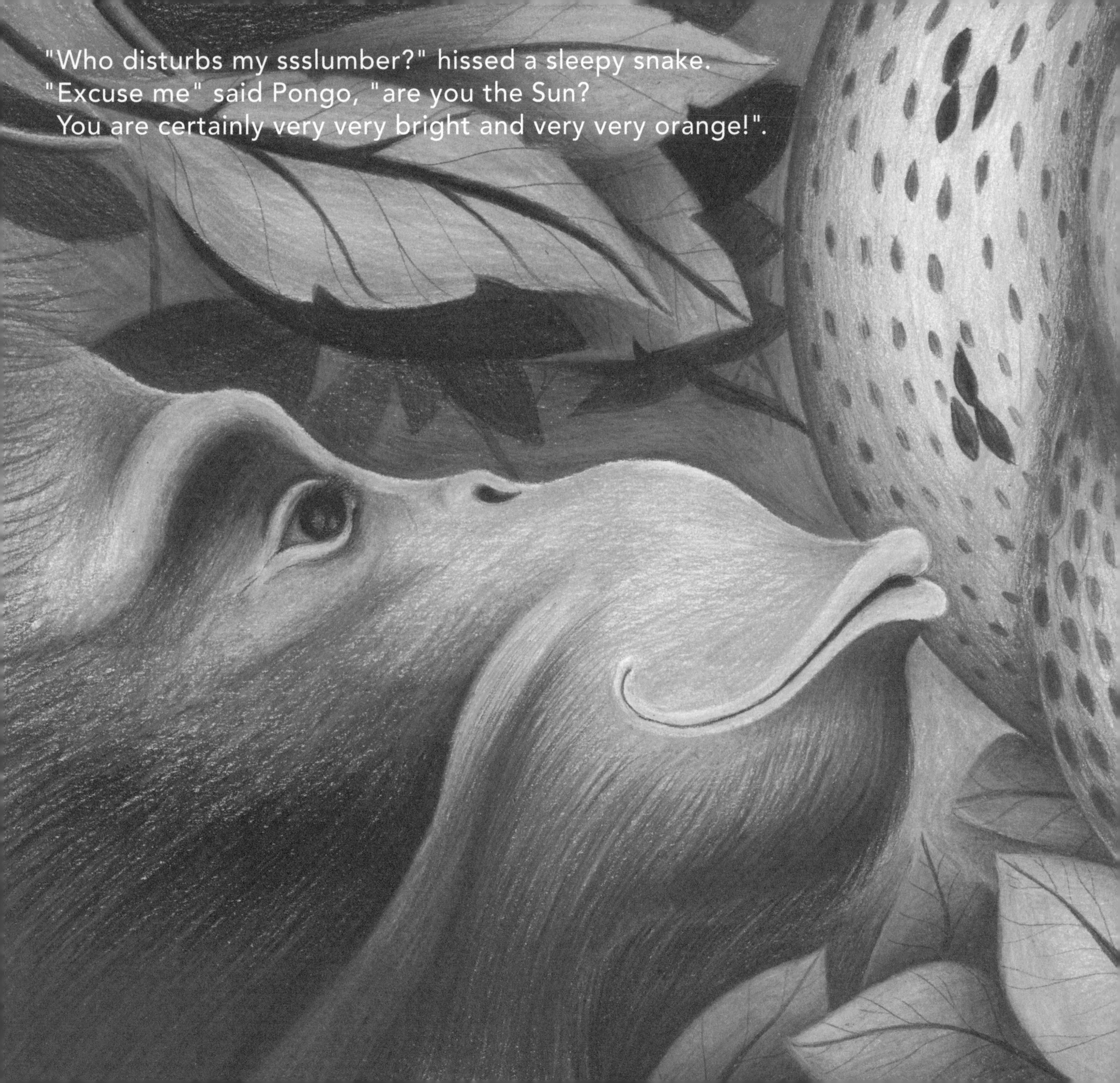

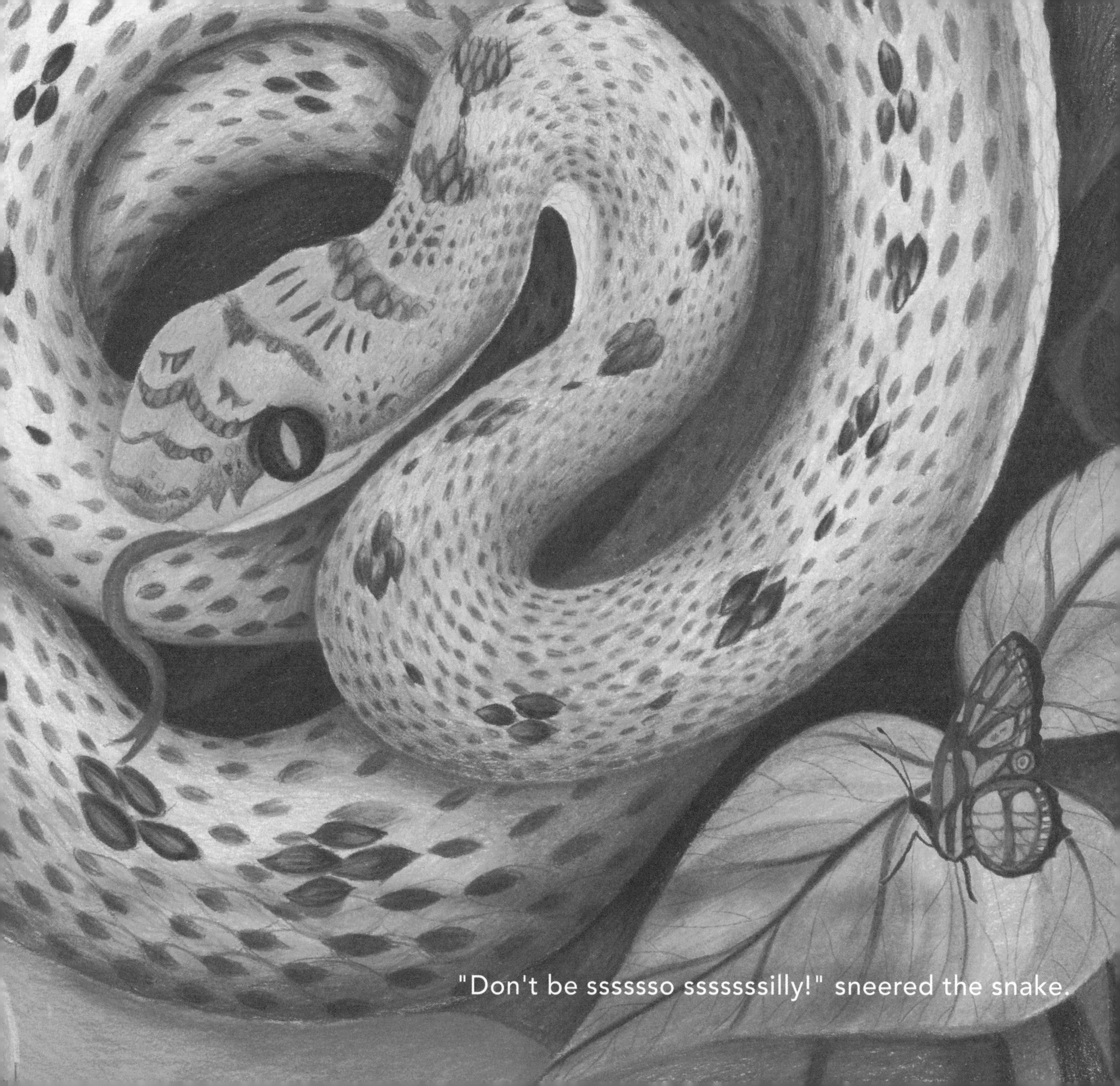

"Don't be ssssso sssssssilly!" sneered the snake.

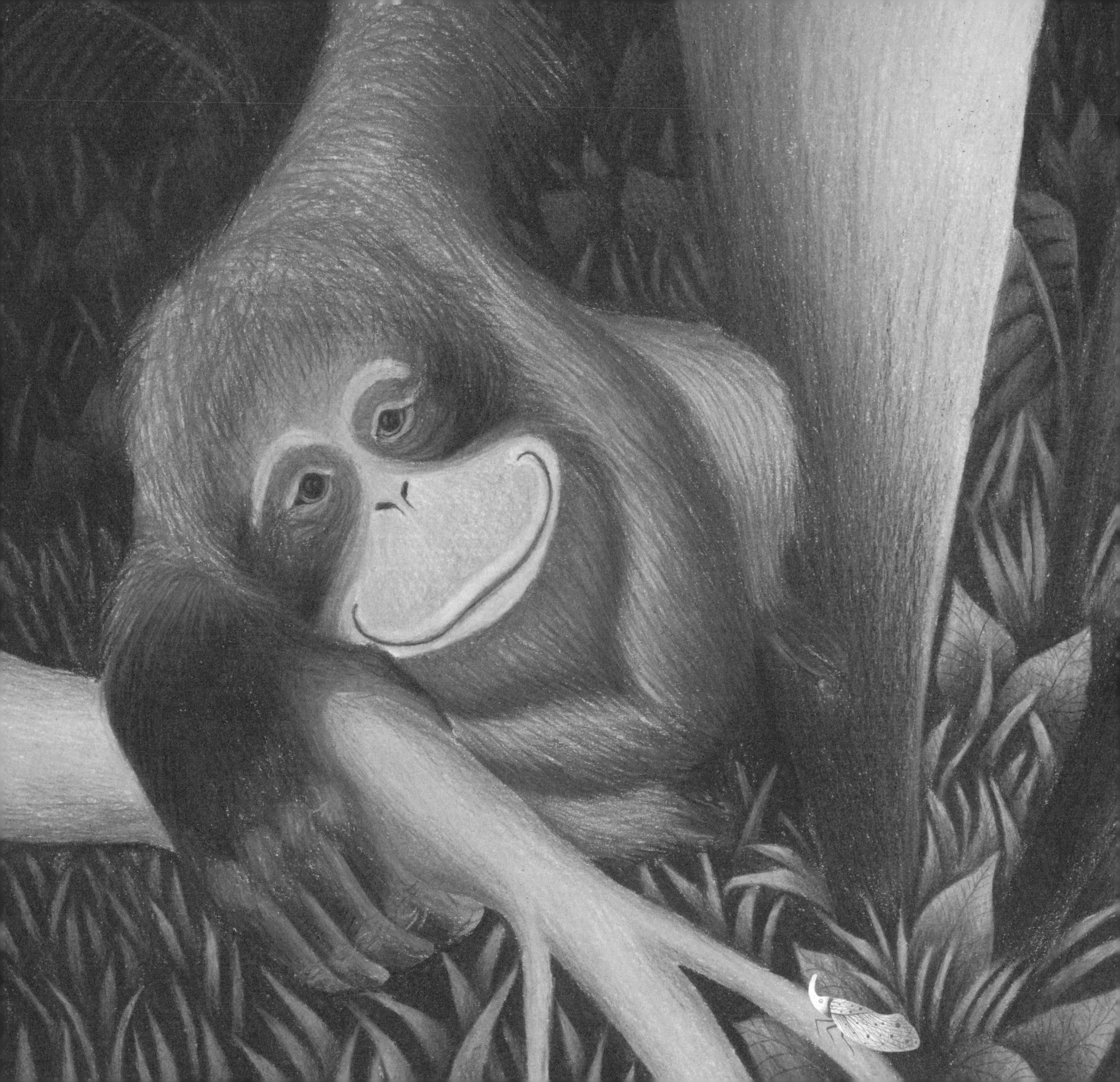

Pongo climbed higher and higher through the branches, until he was so high up that the snake was just a tiny speck beneath him.

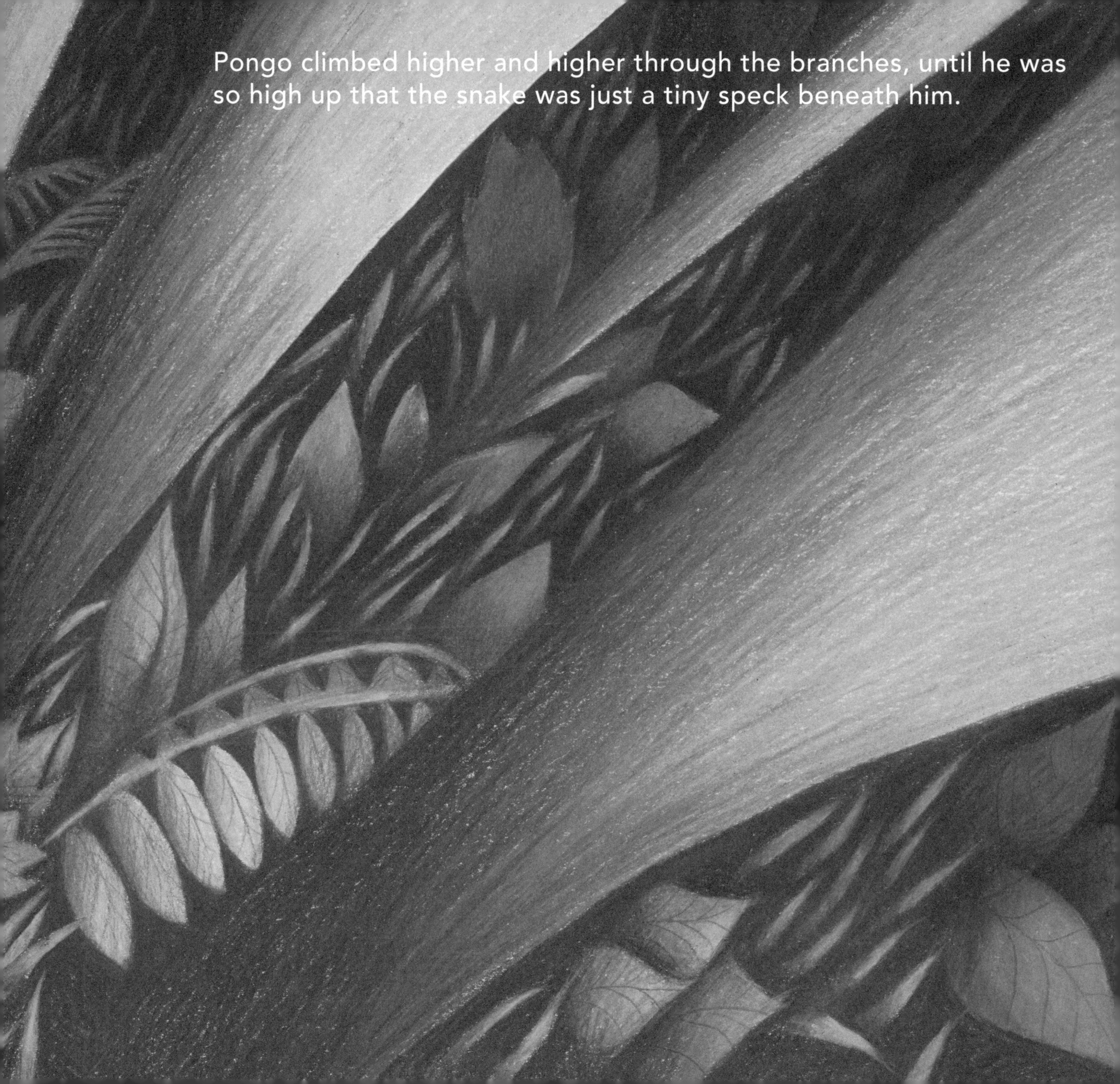

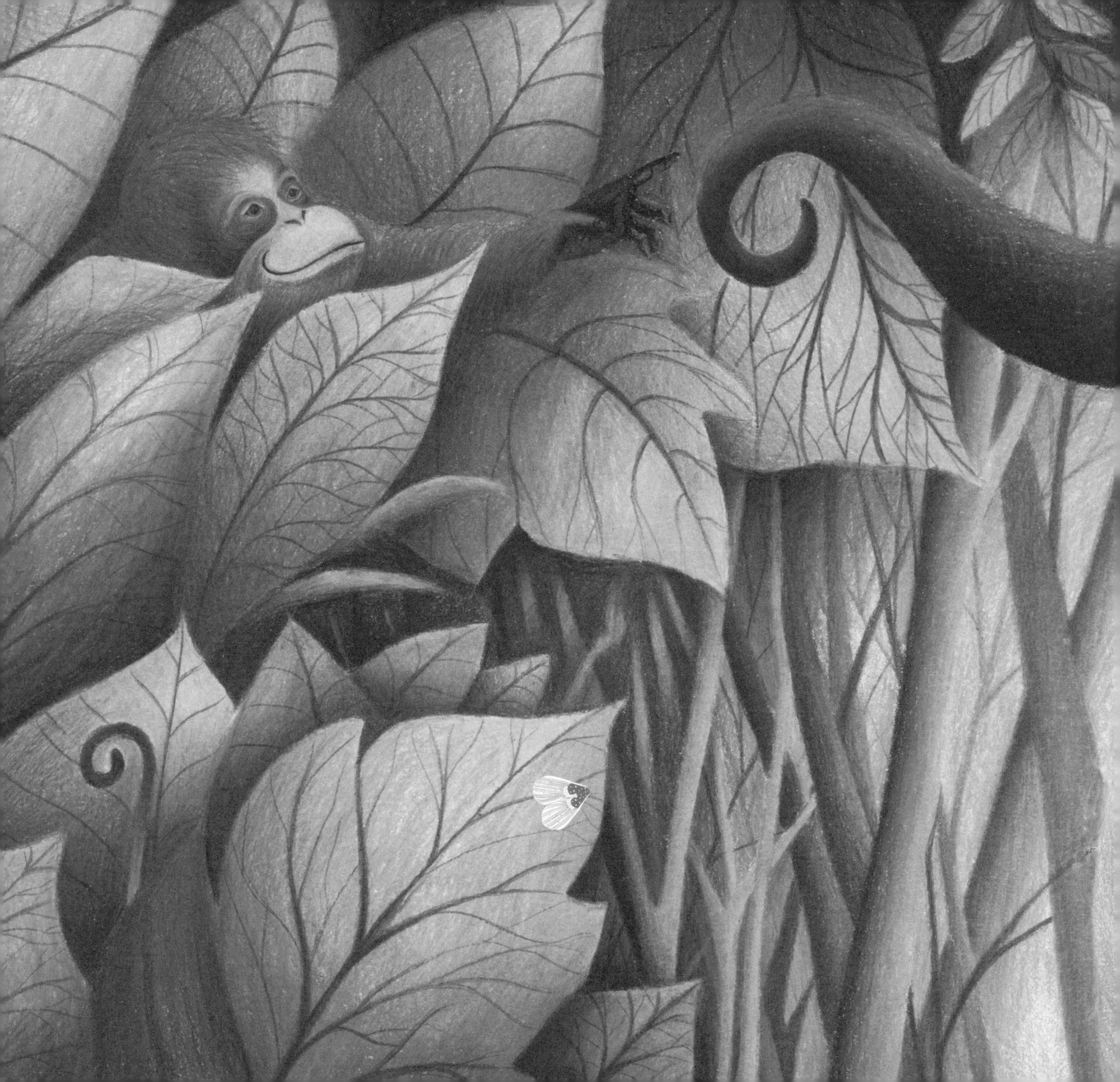

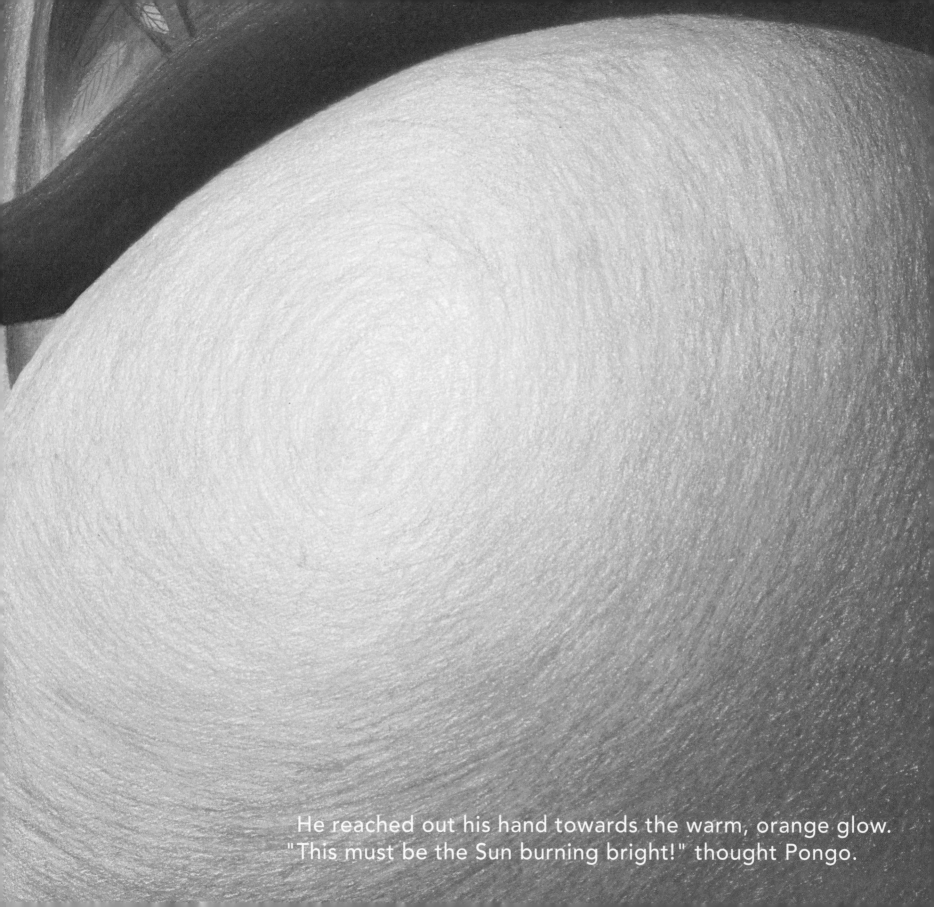

He reached out his hand towards the warm, orange glow.
"This must be the Sun burning bright!" thought Pongo.

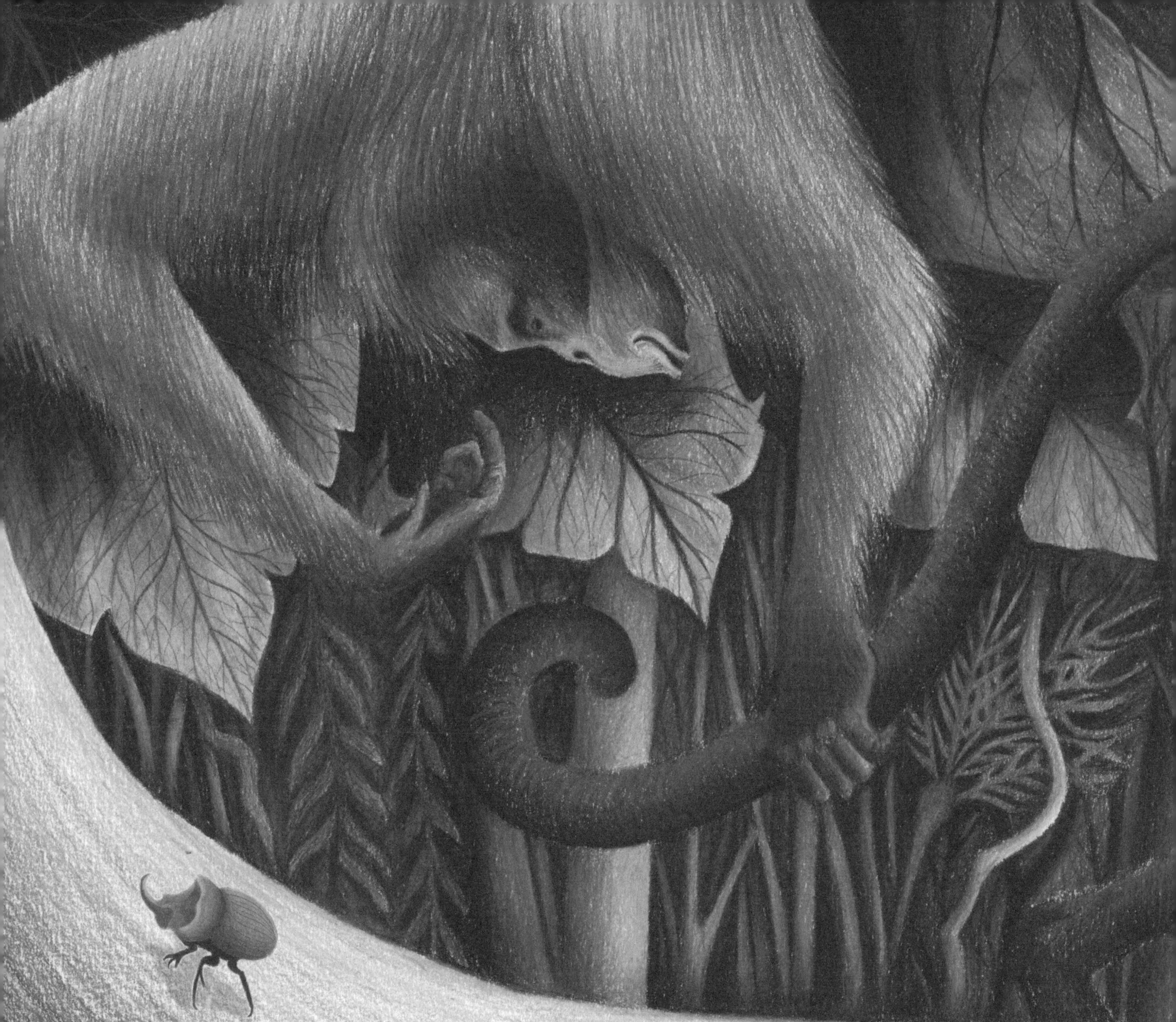

"What do you think you are doing!
Get off my bottom you silly ape!" screeched a furious baboon.

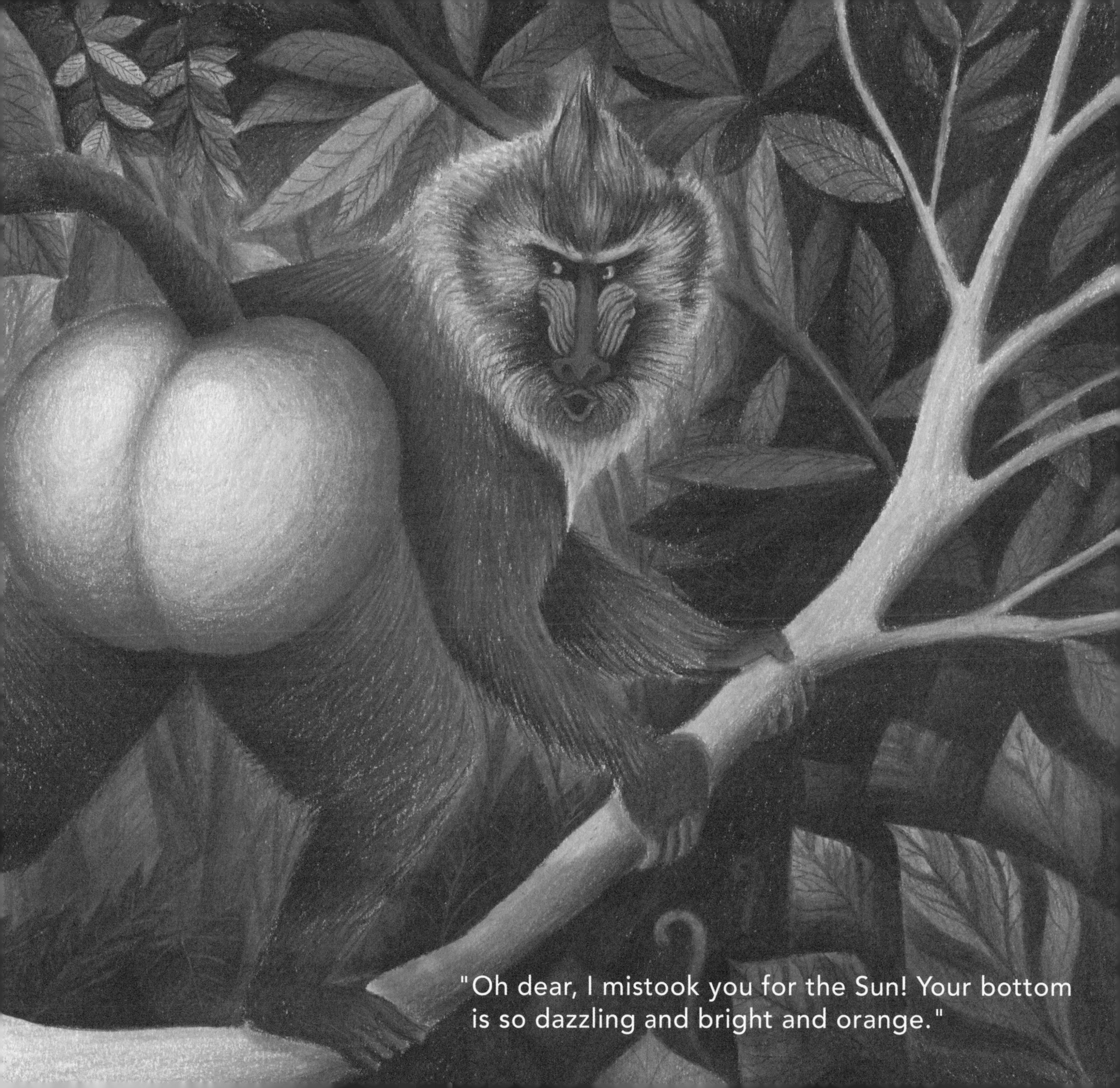

"Oh dear, I mistook you for the Sun! Your bottom is so dazzling and bright and orange."

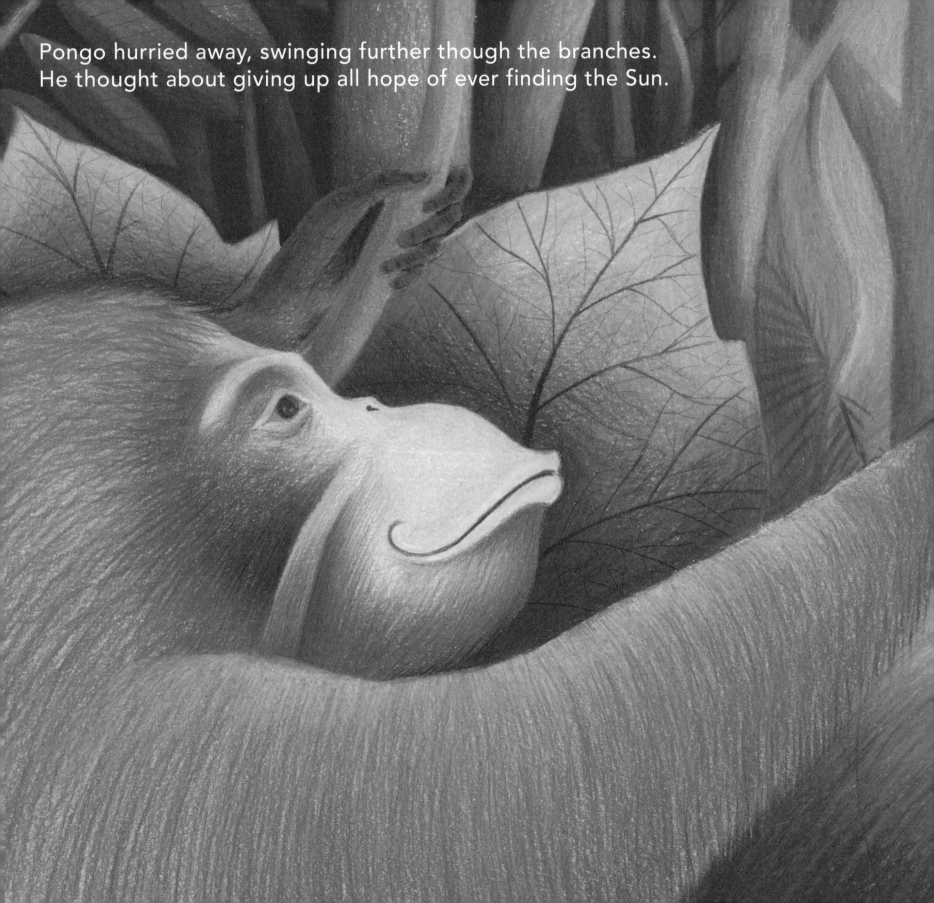

Pongo hurried away, swinging further though the branches.
He thought about giving up all hope of ever finding the Sun.

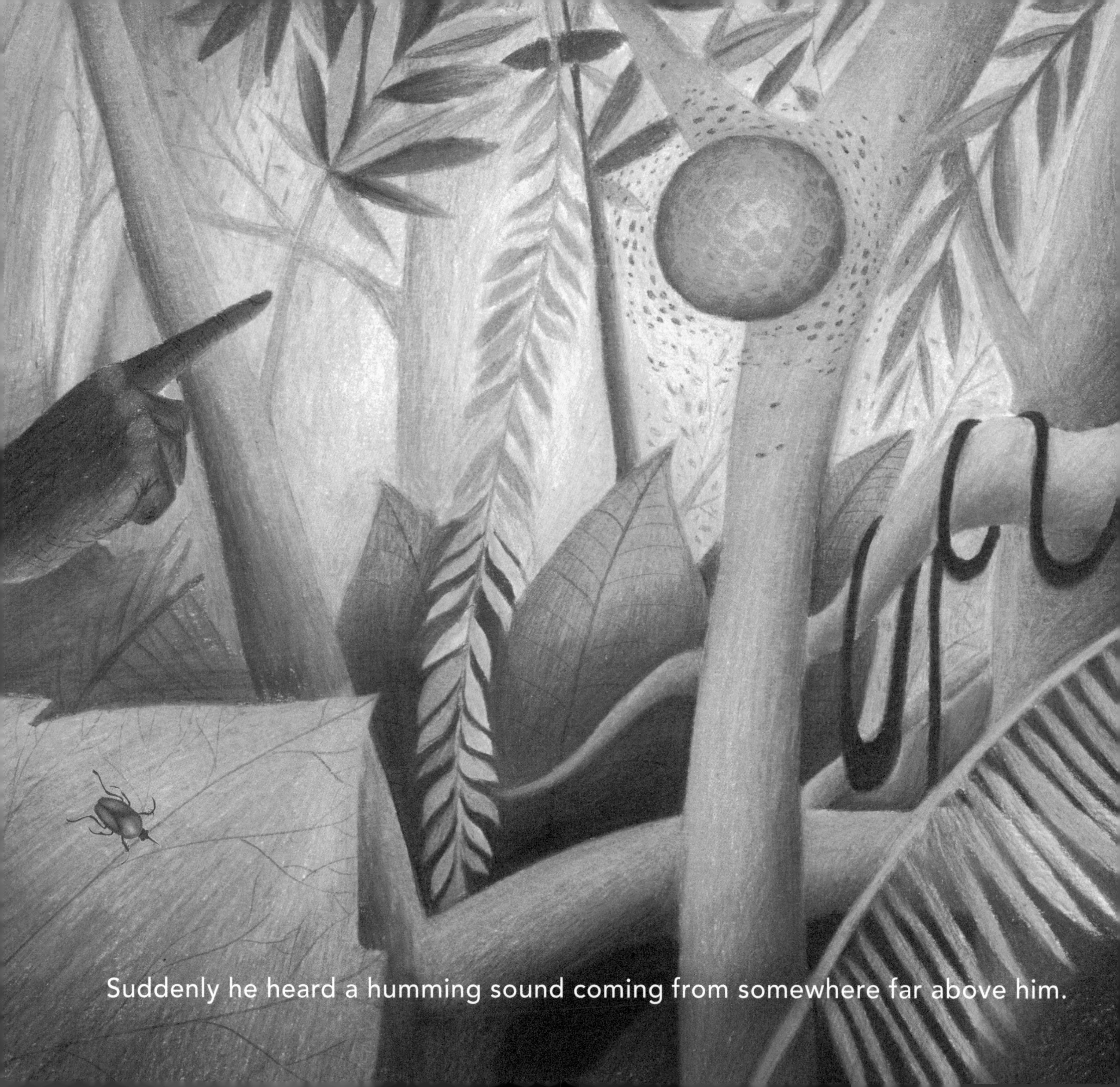

Suddenly he heard a humming sound coming from somewhere far above him.

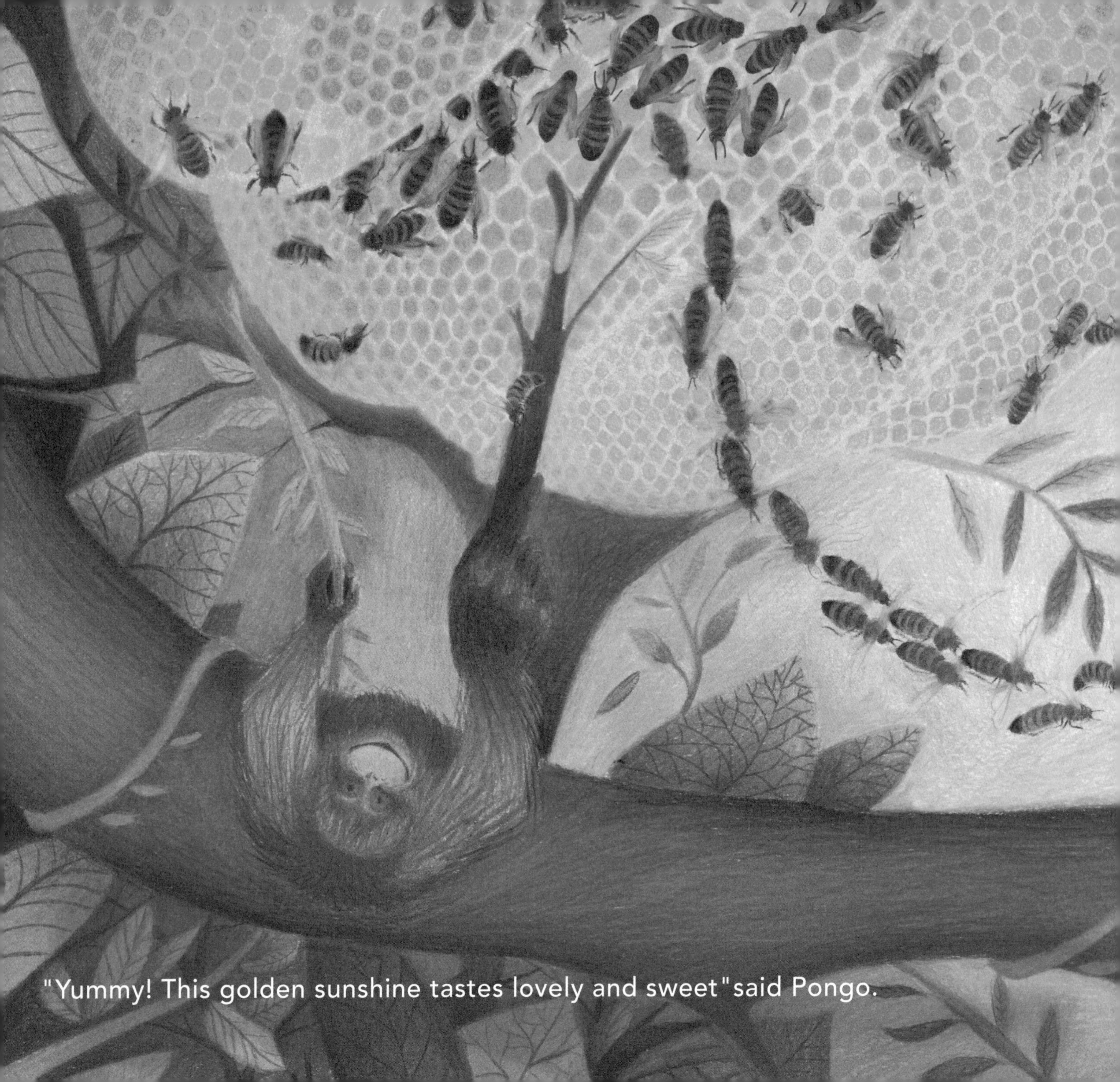

"Yummy! This golden sunshine tastes lovely and sweet"said Pongo.

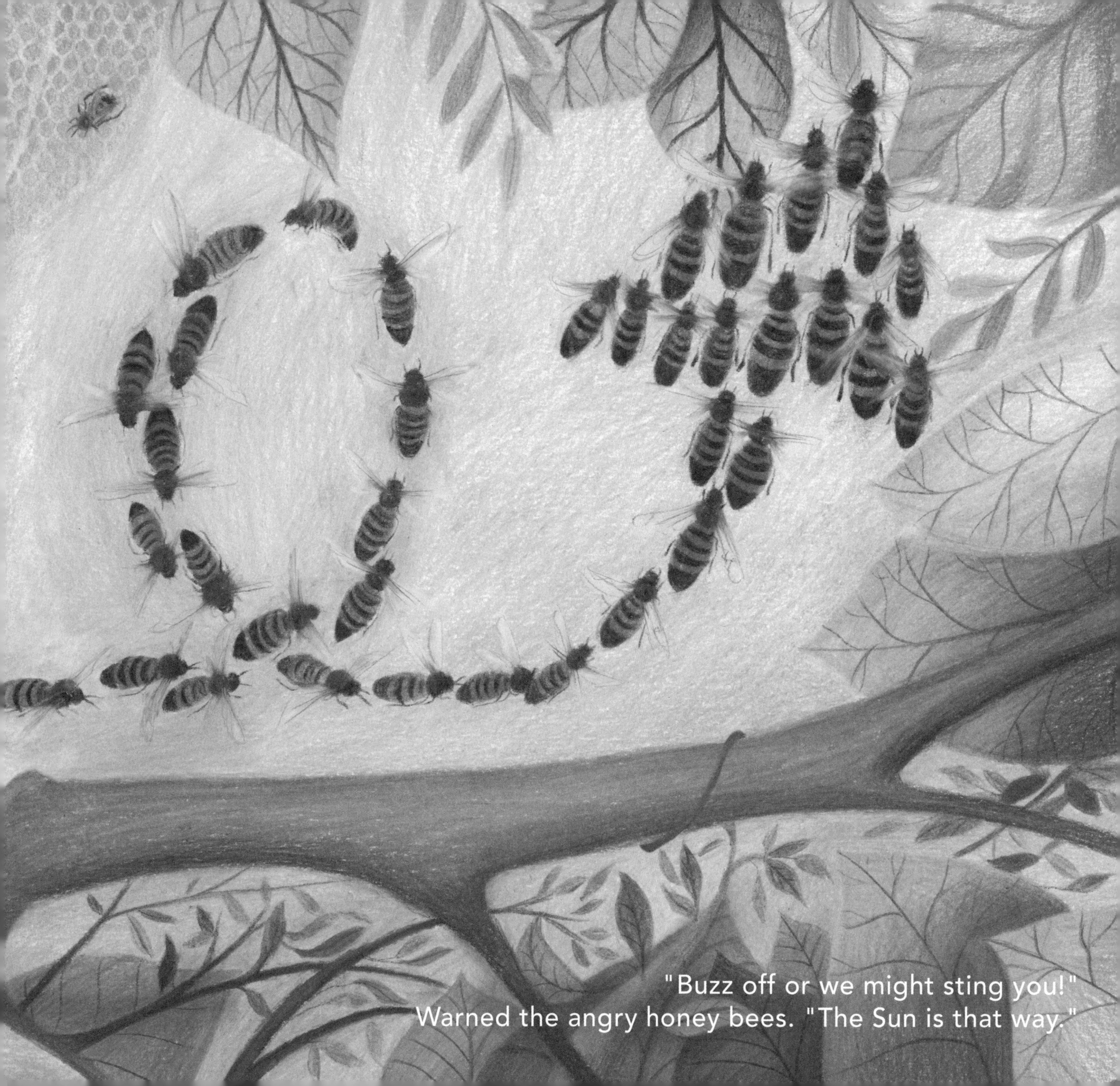

"Buzz off or we might sting you!"
Warned the angry honey bees. "The Sun is that way."

Pongo soared up into the treetops.

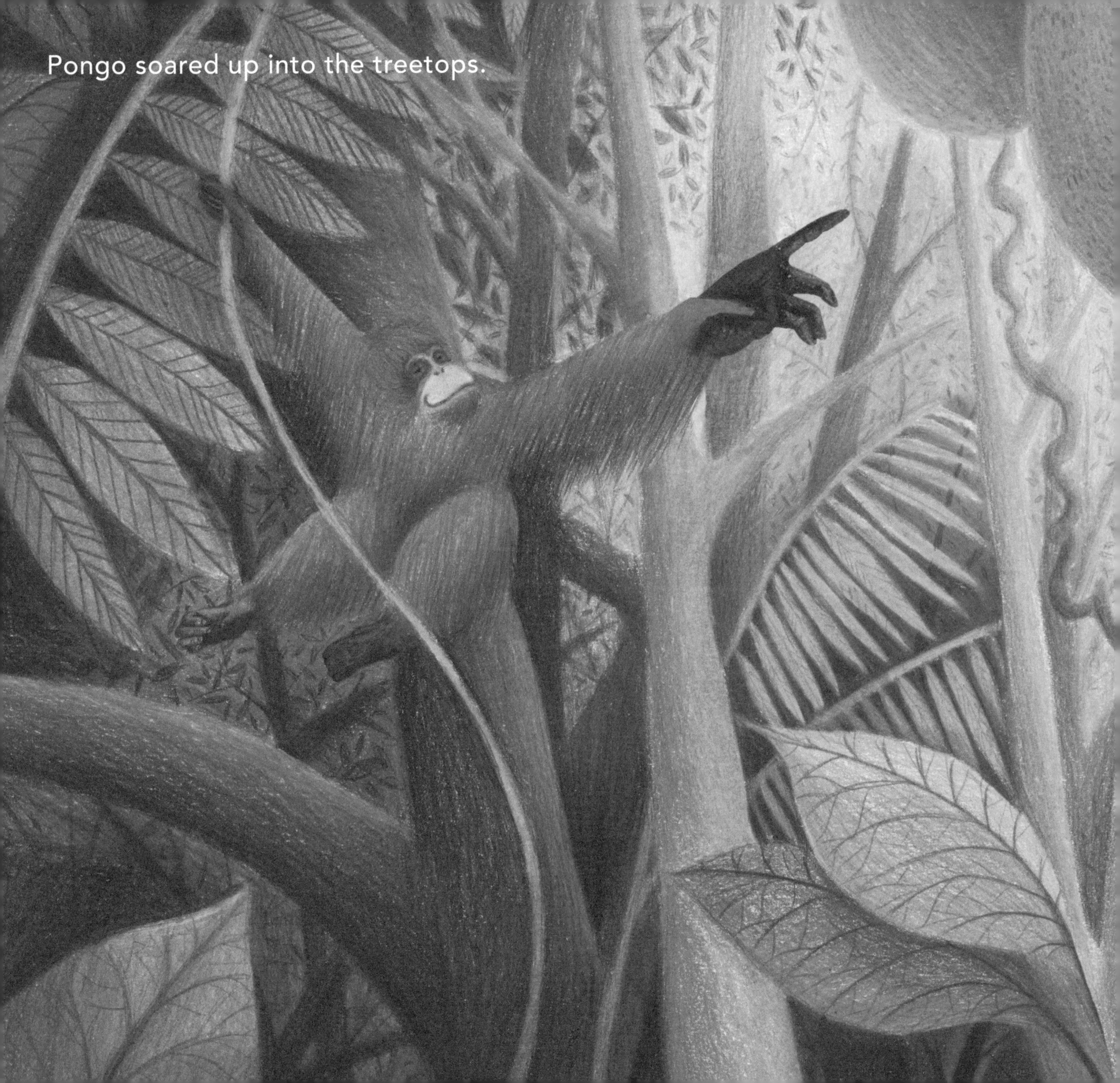

He saw something shimmering in the strong boughs of a tree.

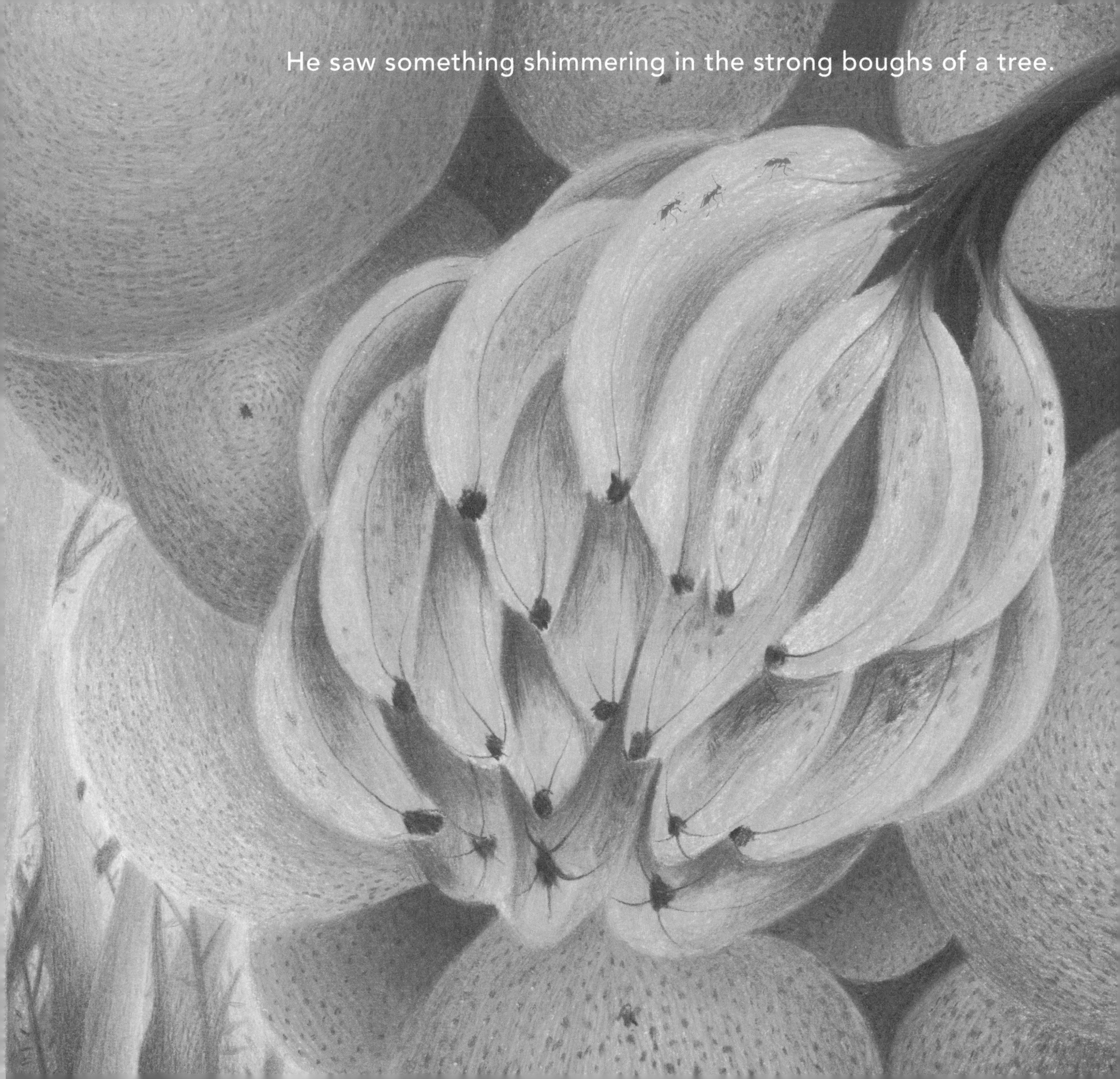

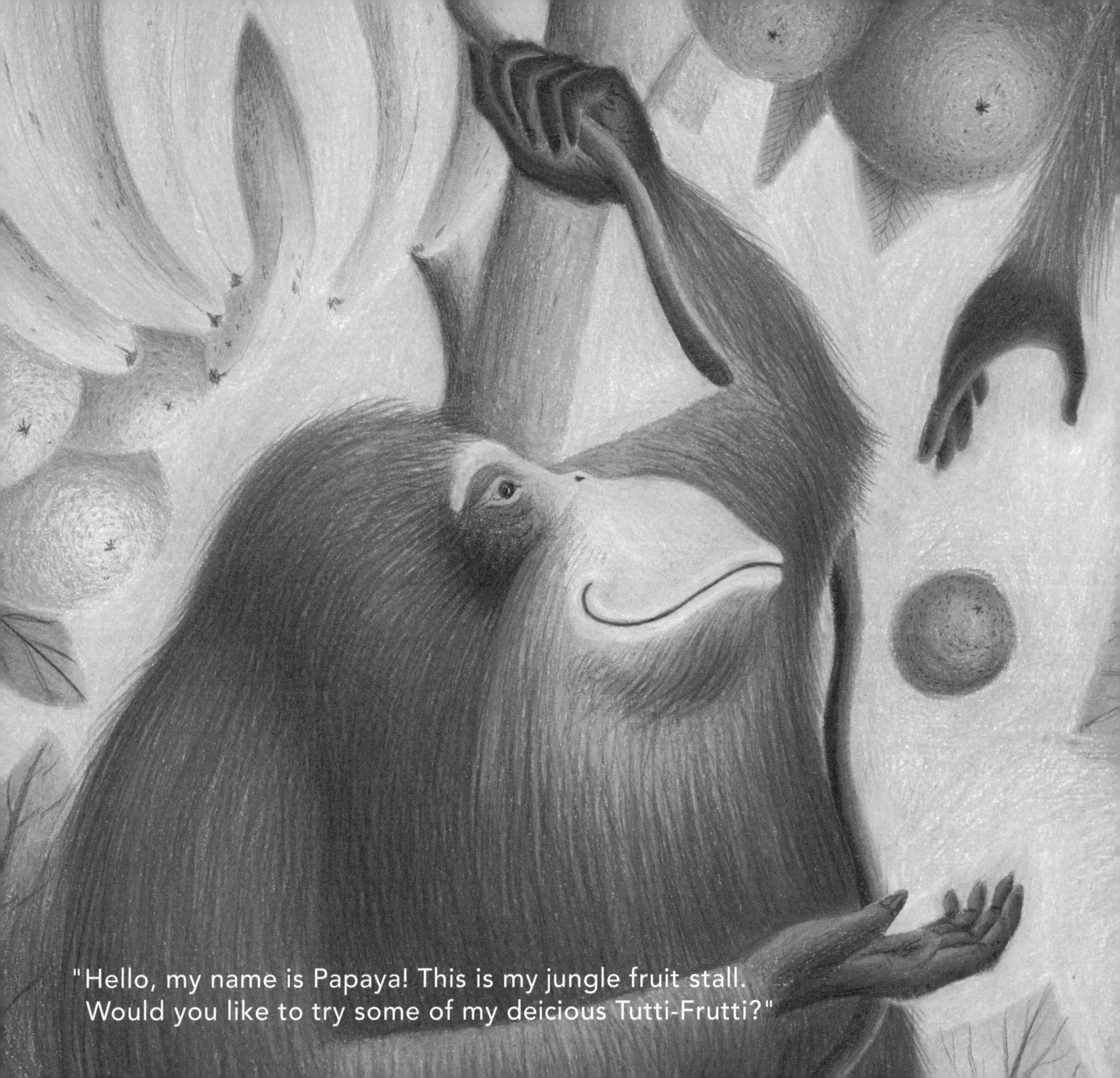

"Hello, my name is Papaya! This is my jungle fruit stall.
Would you like to try some of my deicious Tutti-Frutti?"

As Pongo ate a juicy orange, he told Papaya of his search for the Sun.

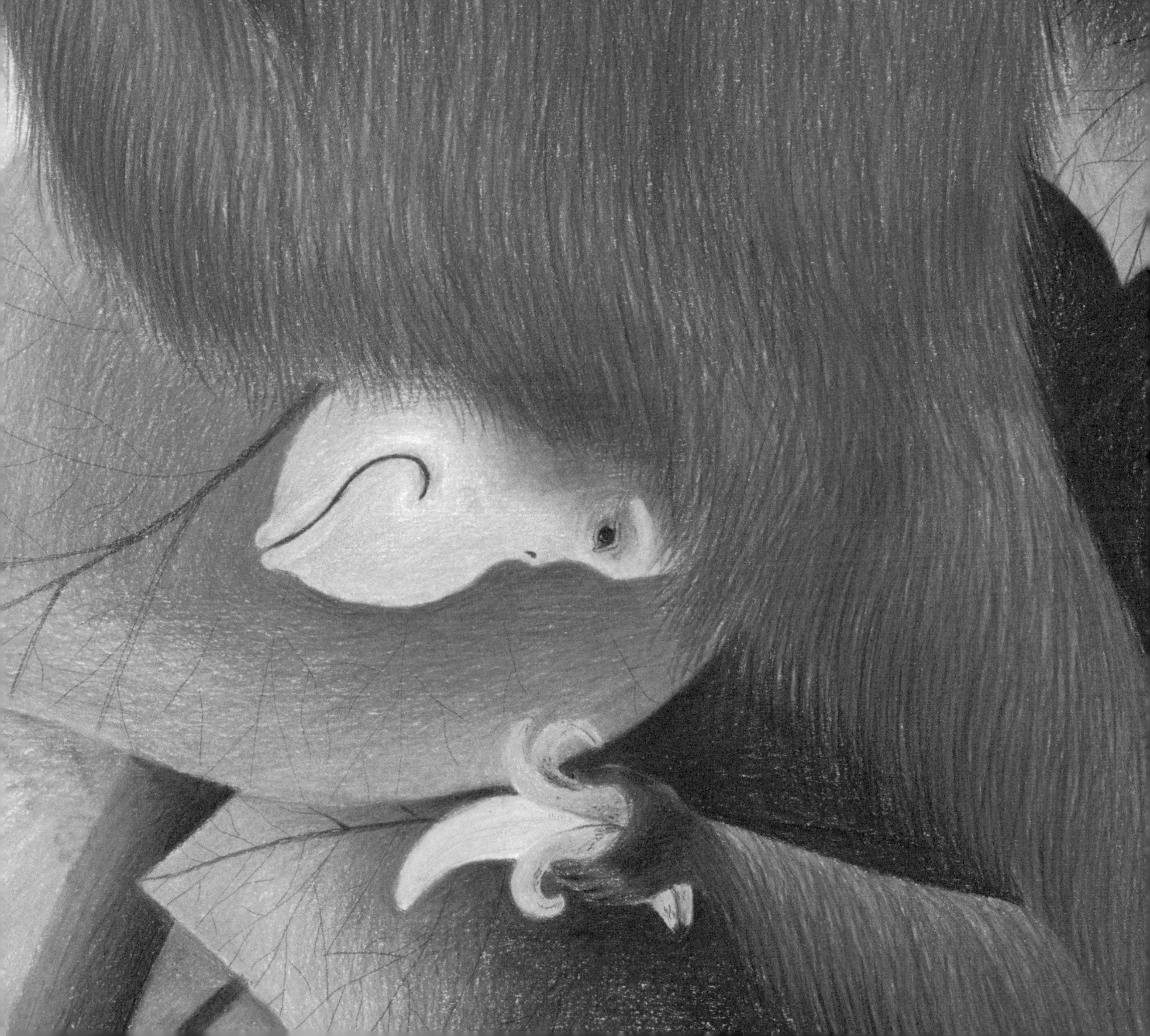

"Follow me" called Papaya as she swung gracefully through the branches, "It's up here". Pongo searched for the bright orange Sun but he could not see it.

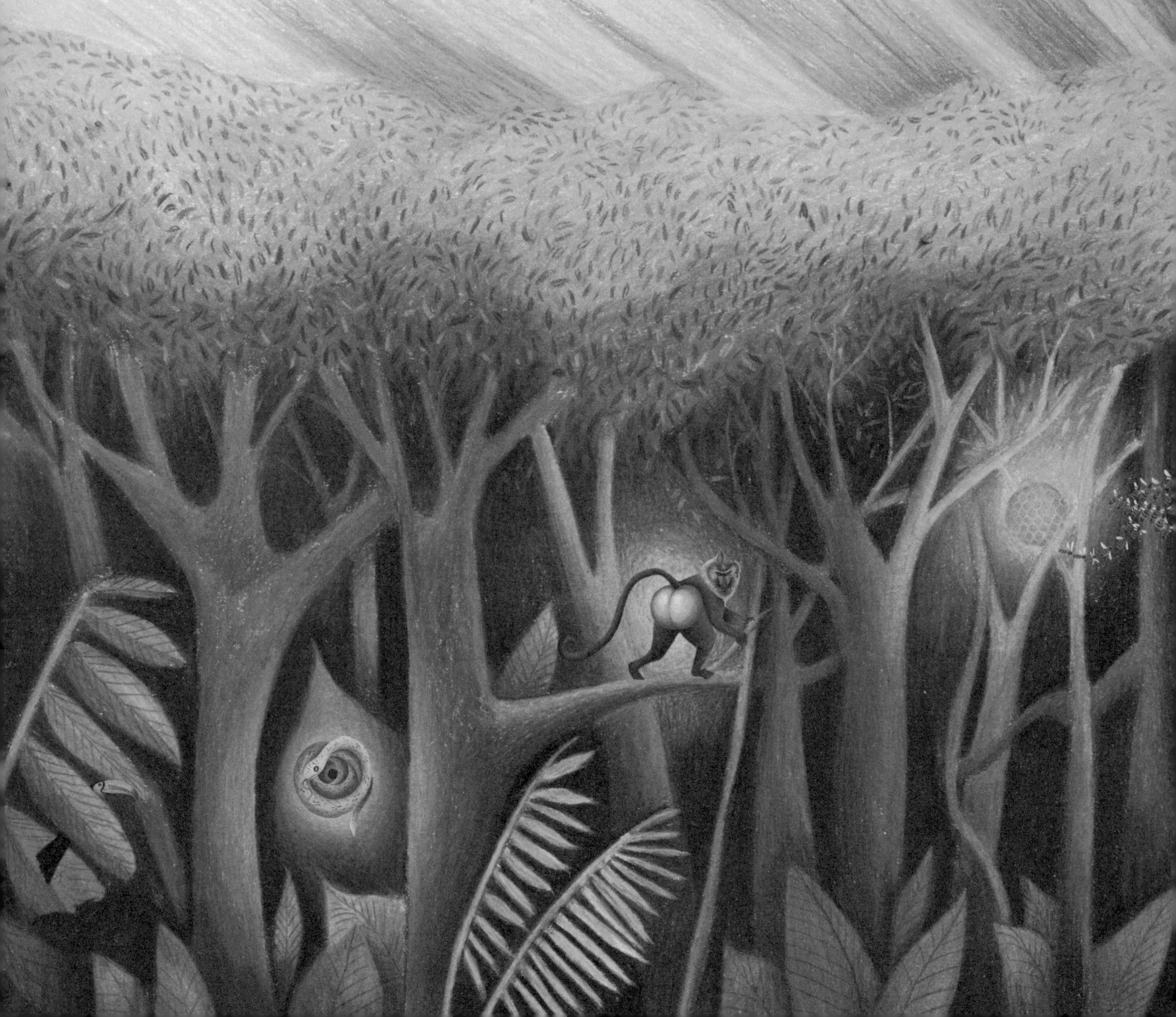

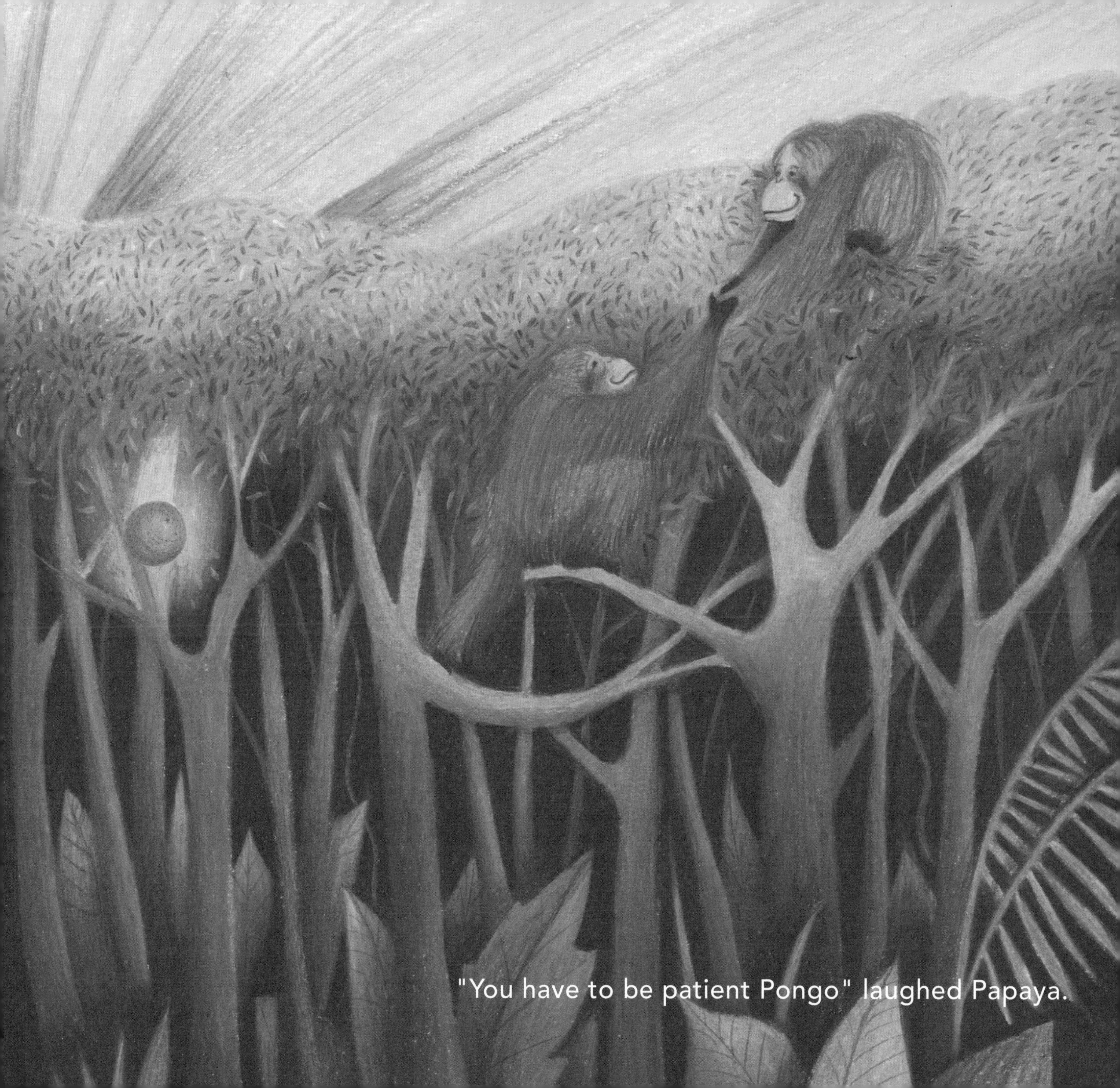

"You have to be patient Pongo" laughed Papaya.

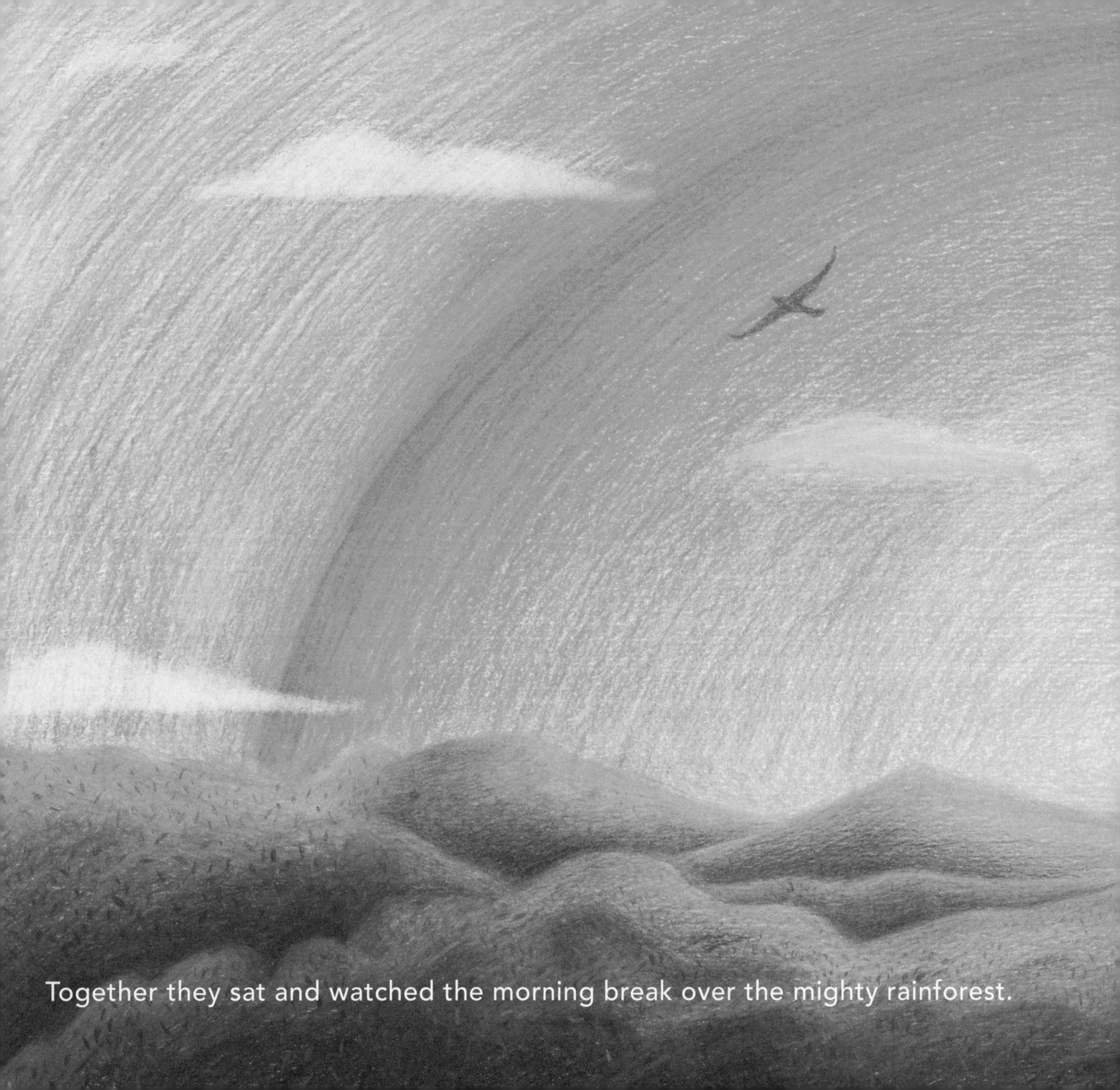

Together they sat and watched the morning break over the mighty rainforest.

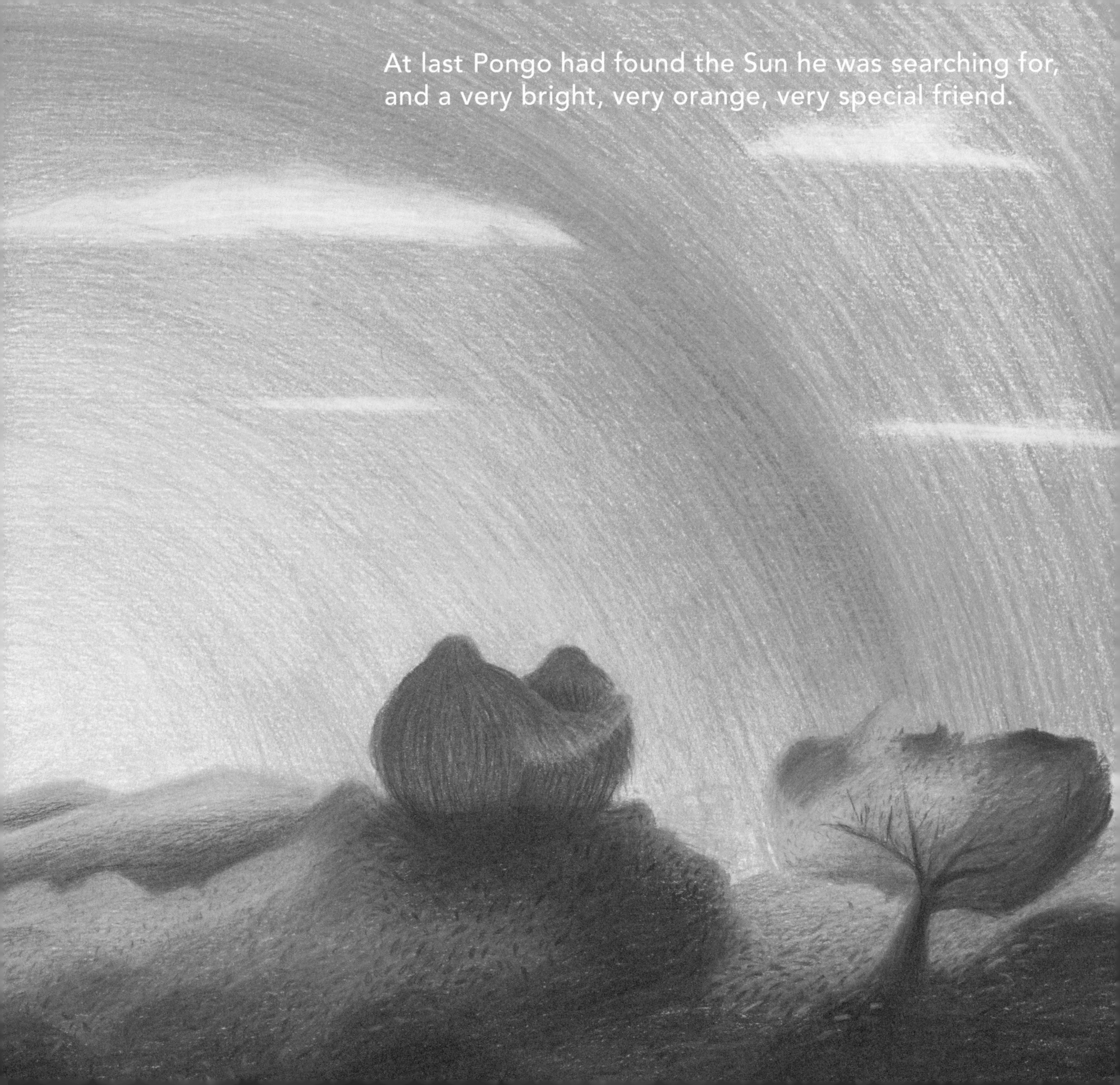

At last Pongo had found the Sun he was searching for,
and a very bright, very orange, very special friend.

Published by Flying Eye Books, an imprint of Nobrow Ltd. 62 Great Eastern Street, London, EC2A 3QR.

ISBN 978-1-909263-09-3

Order from www.flyingeyebooks.com